THE
THIEVES'
MARKET

THE THIEVES' MARKET

by Dennis Haseley

illustrated by Lisa Desimini

HarperCollins*Publishers*

Library of Congress Cataloging-in-Publication Data
Haseley, Dennis.
    The thieves' market / by Dennis Haseley ; illustrated by Lisa
Desimini.
        p.   cm.
    Summary: Children wake in the night and visit the unusual market
where thieves sell their stolen goods.
    ISBN 0-06-022492-4. — ISBN 0-06-022493-2 (lib. bdg.)
    [1. Robbers and outlaws—Fiction.   2. Markets—Fiction.   3. Night—
Fiction.]   I. Desimini, Lisa, ill.   II. Title.
PZ7.H2688Th   1991   90-38440
[E]—dc20   CIP
                                                                 AC

To Sara & Amy
—D.H.

For Andrew,
a very good friend.
—L.D.

IN THE NIGHT, on camels and horses, they bring their stuff. So quiet—I can hardly hear them—they set up market stalls outside my town.

Roland, the milk thief, has four shaggy cows. Arnold steals silk pockets. And Robert McRobert, who has only six teeth, smiles as he sets up his chocolates.

Down the rows of the thieves' market, as the stars come out and the hills disappear in the night, they're setting out boxes with other boxes inside them, and strange hats and maps.

But in the last stall, wearing a baseball cap and one silver earring, the king of the gypsy thieves sits, not smiling, not frowning, behind a table that holds nothing at all.

The police are asleep in their blue pajamas, and the police horses are asleep under their blue blankets, and all our parents are asleep in their beds.

But I'm sitting up like it's morning.

And it's morning for Susan and Tim and the others waking in their beds, slipping out of their covers, going *shhh, shhh*. In our pajamas—some with prints of flowers, some with dancing bears, and some, like mine, with no prints at all—we run out into the night.

Now the clock is striking three as we file past the square and through the town gate where the watchman is snoring. I hold my stone tightly in my hand. When the light is right, it looks like the head of a horse, and there's a little mark where the eye should be. Over the field, the moon's watching with no eye at all.

I stop and let the others walk past me, into the thieves' market.

There's Susan, gliding past Arthur, the art thief, holding a picture she did when she was little. It's supposed to be her, but it's just a ball for the head and sticks coming down for legs.

Arthur blinks and holds up one painting after another while Susan shakes her head. "No," she says. "No, no, not that one," she says again. He shows her a girl's face floating in empty air. And a mother holding a baby. And an old woman stepping into a stream.

Finally, he shows her a dancer standing on her toes, one hand above her head. Susan puts down her picture, and Arthur, the art thief, snatches it up, but Susan doesn't notice. She stares and stares at that painting of a dancer. Slowly, she rises on her toes. And just as slowly, she lifts her arm.

Ahead, the king of the gypsy thieves watches from under the brim of his cap and doesn't frown or smile. I walk on with my stone.

Now I see my best friend, Tim, walking toward Giovanni, the music thief. Tim circles a fat tuba. And cavalry bugles that glow in the dark. He grins into a pair of cymbals, but they make his face look old.

Finally, he stops where a violin hangs from a peg. As he looks up at it, he starts to sing a song. Then he stops all of a sudden. And all over the thieves' market, we stop what we're doing, because all of us know that song. It's the tune we sing to ourselves on the way to school. It's the song we sing when we look into a puddle and see just our faces.

Now Giovanni's whistling that tune. He takes down the violin and hands it to Tim. Tim sighs as he puts it beneath his chin. And he starts to play another song—a song I've never heard.

A tent flaps in the wind, and I walk, not looking back, holding my stone up to the moon. The king of the gypsy thieves sits behind his table that holds nothing. He doesn't frown. He doesn't smile. And suddenly there's a stall I haven't seen before, one that's filled with darkness, darker than the inside of my closet.

Looking in, I see, floating in the air, a thin purple ribbon twice as long as me. I hear a snort; the ribbon moves forward.

I feel on my face a breath as warm as steam from my mother's soup, but with a smell of earth and mud, grass and salt air. And I get a shiver down my spine. A huge shadow moves. I put my stone in my pocket, and I reach for the ribbon and pull myself up, up as if I'm swimming through water. The horse snorts and moves forward with me on his back.

Now we're out in the grass, away from the tents, and the horse starts to trot and I bounce up and down, up and down. I pull on the rein, but that only seems to make him go faster. I lean down and put my hand on his neck. "Hey, boy," I whisper, and I feel his muscles moving under my hand. He whinnies and starts to move faster, away from my friends, through fields I've never seen before. Above me, the whole sky looks like my first gray blanket, floating away behind the moon.

I pull on the ribbon and my arms feel thicker. My feet reach farther down and grip his belly, and I seem to fit into his back. I yell again, and my voice is deeper. Now I'm drumming over the fields, faster and faster, so tall and strong. On the ground I can see each stone, each blade of grass, and I know I need never go back.

But the horse slows, and I'm growing light again, bouncing on his back. And now ahead, I see the tents once again. I ride through the market and the horse stops. I jump down and reach for the old gray stone in my pocket. But it's gone.

The king of the gypsy thieves puts his fingers to his mouth and whistles twice. I look up and see a streak of dawn in the sky.

Back toward the gate of our town we run while the thieves rush around packing up. Over my shoulder, I see them putting on hats and grabbing up chocolates and boxes and maps. In the center of it all, the king of the gypsy thieves takes off his cap and looks right into my eyes. And he smiles.

But from this distance, he looks like a boy, with something in his hand, walking with other children into the night. For a moment, I feel like I'm the one who's tall, tall and strong. And I wonder if he can see my smile.

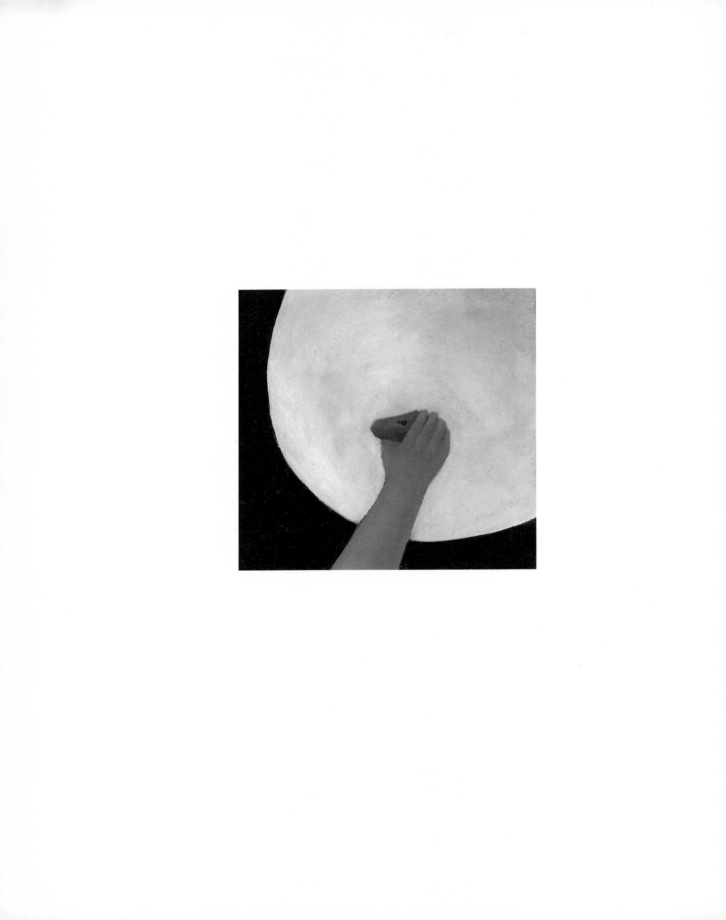